One More Try

Dr. Blake Brandes
Valerie Brender
Lola Svetlova

MotivationalMillennial

Out in a quarry
Hours from town
There lived a gargoyle
Who was feeling down.

One month ago
Her best friend Sand
Left on a quest
To a distant land.

Naomi's Nook

Now she's alone –
No friends around.
It's just her parents
And gnomes underground.

Gardy and Sand
Always felt cool
As the only kids
Being gnome-schooled.

Now that Sand's gone,
Their teacher, Naomi,
Tries to help Gardy
Feel less lonely.

"Take a trek out
As far as you can,
For friends may be found
By sky or by land."

She looks for new friends
When out on a walk.
But she just hears crickets,
And crickets don't talk.

She soars through the trees
And searches the rocks.
But she just sees worms,
And worms don't talk.

Gardy is gloomy,
No friends to be found,
But then she recalls
Tales of a town

Filled with dragons
And mythical creatures
And even a school –
a fantastic feature!

Gardy takes flight,
But she has forgotten
About a rather
Significant problem.

At night she is fine
To fly where she pleases,
But during the daylight
She suddenly freezes.

She arrives at Sprout
As dawn breaks
And quickly realizes
She's made a mistake!

"Oh no," she cries!
"I'm turning to stone.
Look at the time!
I won't make it home."

A school bus passes;
The students are shocked
As they watch Gardy
Turn into a rock.

They come back later,
But Gardy can't talk.
So they decorate her
With sidewalk chalk.

When the sun sets
Gardy wakes up
And smiles to see
Her new makeup.

She begins searching
For her new friends,
But all she finds
Are crickets again.

Suddenly smoke
Appears on a mountain.
One puff! Two puffs!
Gardy starts counting.

She spreads her wings
And flies to the billows.
But when she arrives,
She finds Dragon on pillows.

Her hopeful face
Falls with a sigh,
But she is determined
To try and to try.

The whisper of water
Makes Gardy bolt
Until she sees Otter
Asleep in his holt.

Her lip starts to quiver.
She whispers, "Goodbye."
But she is determined
To try and to try.

House after hut
After cave after burrow –
No one's awake,
Though her search has been thorough.

Her tears start to fall.
It's so hard to try
When no one is there
On land or in sky.

She wanders through woods
With her head hung low.
Is this her fate –
Forever alone?

Until…

A hint of a hark of a hoot of an owl
Hollers and startles her out of her cloud.

"Hello and howdy and how do you do?
My name is Allie. How about you?"

"Oh my, oh my, this is such a surprise —
I've never seen owls with my own eyes!
I've only read about fine feathered friends.
Do you all play when the sun rounds the bend?"

Before Allie answers, there is a smack!
As she is knocked off the branch by a bat.
"I'm terribly sorry, oh what a to-do!
My name is Batilda. How about you?"

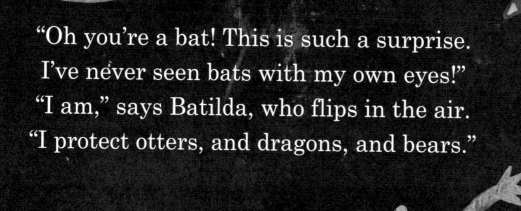

"Oh you're a bat! This is such a surprise.
I've never seen bats with my own eyes!"
"I am," says Batilda, who flips in the air.
"I protect otters, and dragons, and bears."

"You see, we're from Knight School," Allie explains.
"We were just ending our nightly game!
We go on patrols in groups of three."
"But who is your third?"

"Hey, that's me!"

A porcupine rolls into the scene.
"My name is Spines, and I'm leading this team.
We're on a mission to find a weed
That could overrun Sprout if we don't succeed."

"You see," says Spines, "It glows in the dark,
But by day looks like any old plant in the park.
Years ago, it destroyed our town.
We've beaten it back, but it's still around."

"Oh you're a porcupine!" Gardy exclaims.
"My name is Gardy – can I join your game?
I flew from the quarry, hours from town.
I've been looking for friends, but no one's around.

That sounds like a challenge you're facing indeed.
Back in the quarry, we also had weeds:
Giant sunflowers that towered so tall
Until the gnomes got rid of them all."

"Then let us be friends!" Spines replies.
"You're not alone with us by your side.
Come to Knight School, and you will see
Just how amazing a team can be."

Knight School's a-buzz when they all arrive –
Meetings of marvelous moles and mice,
Plenty of possums, and raucous raccoons
Laughing and playing under the moon.

Gardy is joyous, pulled out of her funk,
And welcomed inside by Principal Skunk.
"We're happy you're here and hope that you'll stay."
Gardy has waited so long for this day.

Just then her parents fly down from above,
Embracing their daughter with hugs and love.
"We worried about you and searched all over
Through forests and fields of four-leaf clover."

"Can I go to school here?" Gardy pleads.
"Knight School has so many kids like me."
"We're happy for you that you've found new friends.
We'll check out the options for you to attend."

With family and friends gathered around,
Gardy recounts her trek to the town.
And as she reaches the end of her tale,
She shares how she was afraid she'd fail.

"I tried and I tried,
But I could not find
What I was seeking
Time after time.

Until I tried something
Daring and brave –
Traveling far
Away from my cave."

"I almost lost hope.
I almost gave up.
But one more try
Was exactly enough."

ISBN 978-1-7373128-6-4

First edition January 2024

Motivational Millennial
1750 Lundy Ave
P.O. Box 611028
San Jose, CA 95161
BlakeBrandes.com

Made in the USA
Columbia, SC
28 January 2024

31057107R00018